Megalosaurus

Stegosaurus

KU-409-264

Baryonyx

Styracosaurus

Tyrannosaurus
rex

For Leah and Elsie

First published 2020 by Nosy Crow Ltd
The Crow's Nest, 14 Baden Place
Crosby Row, London SE1 1YW
www.nosycrow.com

ISBN 978 1 78800 572 2(HB)
ISBN 978 1 78800 573 9(PB)

Nosy Crow and associated logos are trademarks
and/or registered trademarks of Nosy Crow Ltd.

Text and illustrations copyright © Penny Dale 2020

The right of Penny Dale to be identified as the author
and illustrator of this work has been asserted.

All rights reserved

This book is sold subject to the condition that it shall not, by way of trade or otherwise, be lent,
hired out or otherwise circulated in any form of binding or cover other than that in which
it is published. No part of this publication may be reproduced, stored in a retrieval system,
or transmitted in any form or by any means (electronic, mechanical, photocopying,
recording or otherwise) without the prior written permission of Nosy Crow Ltd.

A CIP catalogue record for this book is available from the British Library.

Printed in China

Papers used by Nosy Crow are made from wood grown in sustainable forests.

1 3 5 7 9 8 6 4 2 (HB)
1 3 5 7 9 8 6 4 2 (PB)

DINOSAUR CHRISTMAS!

Penny Dale

Stuck Santa Claus calling,
calling Dinosaur Rescue.
Dinosaur Rescue on Christmas Eve!

Help!

Help!

Emergency dinosaurs ready,
ready to rescue Santa.
To rescue Santa
before it's too late!

Brrmmm!

Brrmmm!

Busy dinosaur snow-ploughing,
snow-ploughing the winding road.
The winding road, **on and on.**

Crunch!

Crunch! Crunch!

Excited dinosaurs whizzing,
whizzing on the snowmobiles.
On the snowmobiles,
through the trees.

Rescue dinosaurs zooming,
zooming over the water.
Over the water on the hovercraft.

Whoosh!

Chugga!

Careful dinosaur searching,
searching for Santa's house.
Santa's house . . .
there, in the snow!

Chugga!

Chugga!

Team dinosaur arriving,
arriving and starting to dig.
Starting to dig out Santa's sleigh.

Tractor dinosaur **towing**,
towing Santa's sleigh.
Santa's sleigh that's **stuck** in snow.

Heave!

Helicopter dinosaurs lowering,
lowering down the presents.
The presents to put in Santa's sleigh.

Happy Santa Claus flying,
flying through the sky.
Through the sky with his reindeer.

Joyful dinosaurs playing,
playing and getting ready.
Getting ready for Christmas day . . .